WARRIORS!
MIGHTY FIGHTING MACHINES

Thanks to the creative team:
Senior Editor: Alice Peebles
Design: www.collaborate.agency
Consultant: John Haywood

Hungry Tomato™
A division of Lerner Publishing Group, Inc.
241 First Avenue North
Minneapolis, MN 55401 USA

For reading levels and more information, look up this title at www.lernerbooks.com.

Main body text set in Bell MT.
Typeface provided by Monotype.

Library of Congress Cataloging-in-Publication Data

Chambers, Catherine, 1954– author.
  Mighty fighting machines / by Catherine Chambers ; illustrated by Martin Bustamante.
      pages cm
  Includes bibliographical references and index.
  Audience: Ages 8-12.
  ISBN 978-1-4677-9358-2 (lb : alk. paper) — ISBN 978-1-4677-9601-9 (pb : alk. paper) — ISBN 978-1-4677-9602-6 (eb pdf)
  1. Military weapons—History—Juvenile literature.
  2. Vehicles, Military—History—Juvenile literature. I. Bustamante, Martin, illustrator. II. Title.
  UF500.C415 2016
  623.4—dc23
                                        2015033935

**Manufactured in the United States of America
1 – VP – 12/31/15**

WARRIORS!
MIGHTY FIGHTING MACHINES

by Catherine Chambers
Illustrated by Martín Bustamante

HUNGRY TOMATO™

CONTENTS

Introduction   6

Charging Chariots   8
Fast, furious warfare on ancient battlefields

Shattering Battering Ram   10
Ripping through gates and ramparts

Blasting Ballista   12
A mammoth crossbow targeting the foe

Soaring Siege Towers   14
Mighty structures for storming castles

Terrifying Trebuchet   16
Launching molten missiles and severed heads

Gruesome Greek Fire   18
A flaming terror from the earliest times

Booming Medieval Bombard   20
The merciless mortar that ended an empire

Crushing Cannon   22
Destroying ships and razing cities

Tank Attack!   24
The ultimate battlefield vehicle

Silent, Sinister Submarines   26
Waging secret war in the deep ocean

Into Battle with Mighty Machines   28

More Ferocious Facts and Glossary   30

Index   32

INTRODUCING MIGHTY FIGHTING MACHINES

In ancient times, conflicts were long and brutal. Rulers and generals were looking for ways to shorten battles and bring speedy victories. Mighty fighting machines provided the answer. As William Tecumseh Sherman (1820–1891), general in the Union Army in the American Civil War, declared,

"A battery of field artillery is worth a thousand muskets."

CHANGES IN WARFARE

Once, when armies marched across vast plains and deserts, soldiers carried their own weapons, throwing them or wielding them in hand-to-hand combat with the enemy. Warfare began to change perhaps as early as 2800 BCE, when the Sumerians (who lived in the area of modern Iraq) introduced four-wheeled wagons drawn by donkeys. These lumbering vehicles led to quicksilver war chariots pulled by strong, nimble horses—one of the first mighty fighting machines.

Advances in science led to the discovery of gunpowder. Developments in metal smelting and casting technology allowed bigger and better shooting machines. And so, fighting with mighty machines became normal in warfare. Armor and fortifications also strengthened as the size and power of weapons increased.

Modern tanks can be fitted with rockets, anti-aircraft guns, and powered guided missiles. Anti-tank rockets and buried mines have been developed to stop advancing tanks.

Siege of Stirling Castle 1304

Battle of Liège 1914

Siege of Tyre 332 BCE

Battle of Cambrai 1917

Battle of Kadesh 1274 BCE

Defeat of the Spanish Armada 1588

Submarine activity during World War I

Siege of Jerusalem 70 CE

Siege of Rhodes 305 CE

Siege of Constaninople 1453

GREAT WALLS FACING GREATER WEAPONS

As cities grew, great walls were built around them for protection. Attacking armies developed ever more destructive weapons to break them down. Siege warfare had begun. The besieged defenders pushed back their attackers with fire and huge boulders. Attackers pounded fortress walls with destructive machines that could catapult heavy missiles from afar.

A deep, wide moat was dug around 14th-century Bodiam Castle in southern England. Mighty catapults and ballistas were designed to fire missiles with force across waters such as these.

MIGHTY ARMIES FOR MIGHTY MACHINES

A huge army of soldiers and craftsmen was required to attack successfully on land using massive machinery. Carpenters and joiners assembled great wooden catapults. Blacksmiths made sure that cannon were fitted together securely. Hundreds, sometimes even thousands, of troops were needed to move giant siege towers. Teams of horses pulled the biggest, heaviest cannon into position. And all this time, the armies preparing for battle needed protection from the enemy they faced. So hundreds of armed troops gathered at the ready to defend them.

About 8,000 life-size terracotta soldiers were modeled and buried over 2,000 years ago in a Chinese emperor's tomb. There were also 130 models of chariots, one of the first-ever mighty fighting machines.

GREAT BATTLES

At the Battle of Kadesh, fought between Egypt and the Hittites in 1274 BCE, the Hittites' chariots rammed two Egyptian divisions. But the Egyptians surprised them with other units. Both sides declared victory!

TOP TACTICS

Chariot tactics varied widely. Chariot units could use their speed to split an oncoming infantry formation, scattering its soldiers. The chariots' archers then easily picked off the disordered enemy.

MAKING THE MACHINE

Chariots were developed to run on two lightweight spoked wheels. The carriage platform and frame were made of wood. The frame was covered in lightweight wickerwork or leather.

FEROCIOUS FACTS

● Hittites came from around the area of modern Turkey. They used chariots to build one of the greatest empires in the Middle East.

● Assyrian kings from 900–700 BCE showed their power by leading their brutal armies on chariots.

CHARGING CHARIOTS

Terrifying war chariots helped kingdoms expand into empires. Early chariots were heavy, built to ram and crush their opponents. Later designs were lightweight and fast, and could sweep across grassland steppe and desert. All needed horses bred to be strong enough to pull them. Many armies, such as the Hyksos of the Middle East, improved their designs. Chariots' impact at speed was devastating. They surrounded the enemy or darted in and out of battle, attacking from a safe distance. On the chariot, one or more soldiers threw javelins or shot arrows from powerful bows.

WHERE
From Asia in the East to Celtic Europe in the West

WHEN
About 1800 BCE– 300s CE

SHATTERING BATTERING RAM

WHERE
From China, through
the Mediterranean, to
Western Europe

WHEN
About
2000 BCE–1500 CE

The battering ram was the first great siege engine. It extended warfare from open landscapes to heavily fortified castles and cities. This gigantic weapon splintered fortress gates and demolished city walls and bridges. Early rams were massive tree trunks, with metal wrapped around their sharpened ends. Later, soldiers maneuvered the ram inside a lightweight wooden cage set on wheels. The tree trunk was suspended from the cage's roof by chains or ropes. From these it could be swung back and forth, the blade end repeatedly hitting its target with great force.

GREAT BATTLES

At the Siege of Tyre in 332 BCE, Alexander the Great mounted battering rams on his ships to shatter the island city's walls. A long gangplank carried his soldiers over the rubble.

TOP TACTICS

Soldiers aimed the battering ram at the corners of castles so that two walls were breached at once. This made both walls very unstable and opened up a larger gap for infantry to enter.

MAKING THE MACHINE

The wooden cage was roofed with wet leather to shield it from burning missiles thrown from fortress ramparts. In later models, pulleys and levers moved the ram into the best position.

FEROCIOUS FACTS

• The ax-like blade of the battering ram was rammed between stones and then levered so that it pulled the wall apart.

• These terrifying siege weapons measured 20–125 ft (6–38 m) long.

GREAT BATTLES

At the Siege of Jerusalem in 70 CE, Roman artillery pounded the city walls. A single-armed ballista hurled stones weighing up to 55 lb (25 kg).

TOP TACTICS

An army's first line of attack against a fortification was its battalion of ballistas. It aimed to neutralize defenders up in the ramparts while siege weapons such as the battering ram were mounted.

MAKING THE MACHINE

A ballista's ropes could be made from animal sinew or human hair. Patriotic women of ancient Greece grew their hair long especially for them. A strong wood or metal frame housed the mechanism.

FEROCIOUS FACTS

• The largest ballista could accurately blast a 60-lb (27-kg) missile up to 1,500 ft (455 m).

• A small, single-armed metal ballista fired so fast it could pierce through two soldiers with one bolt.

• Ancient Greeks fired flaming bolts.

BLASTING BALLISTA

This spring-mounted siege machine was like a giant crossbow. It fired sharpened poles, metal bolts, and stones with great force. Unlike the battering ram, the ballista targeted people more than structures. Its missiles were aimed by both the attackers and defenders of a fortification. At times, ballistas were lined up to fire at troops in the field. To blast weapons from a ballista, soldiers pulled back two firing arms with tightly twisted cords attached to them. When the cords were released they acted like springs. Army engineers built ballistas to order where they were needed.

WHERE
Middle East, Mediterranean, and Western Europe

WHEN
About 400 BCE–1300 CE

SOARING SIEGE TOWERS

WHERE
China, Middle East,
Mediterranean, and
Western Europe

WHEN
About 1000 BCE–
1500s CE

The enormous siege tower enabled troops to attack and storm fortifications at close range. Hundreds or even thousands of troops wheeled or rolled this column of platforms into place, often over rubble-filled moats. A battering ram on the lower platforms penetrated the stone walls, sometimes aided by drills. The stories above teemed with archers showering arrows upward through slits at the defending enemy, pushing them back. At this point, a hinged bridge at the top of the siege tower was lowered onto the ramparts. From here, the attacking battalions stormed the fortification.

GREAT BATTLES

In 305 CE, King Demetrius I of Macedonia besieged the island state of Rhodes with his greatest tower, the Helepolis. It was protected with iron plates. Soldiers fired missiles through its shuttered holes.

TOP TACTICS

Siege towers were positioned to protect troops climbing up ladders toward the ramparts. Later, when guns overtook arrows, armies adapted the structures to hold cannon, creating battery towers.

MAKING THE MACHINE

A siege tower was built on site with wood. It was usually topped with soaked leather to quench enemy firebombs. Romans used wickerwork or wooden shields to protect the structure.

FEROCIOUS FACTS

● At the Siege of Kenilworth Castle in England in 1266, a single tower housed 200 archers and 11 great catapults.

● Helepolis, the name of King Demetrius I's siege tower, means "Taker of Cities." It was nine stories high, and 3,400 soldiers were needed to move it.

GREAT BATTLES

In 1304, King Edward I of England laid siege to Stirling Castle in Scotland. He attacked the fortifications with a monumental trebuchet called Warwolf, which could launch 300-lb (136-kg) missiles.

TOP TACTICS

The trebuchet was a weapon of fear. It hurled boiling tar and hot sand that burned soldiers under their metal armor. The enemy was also bombarded with beehives, carcasses of diseased cattle, and the severed heads of captives.

MAKING THE MACHINE

The trebuchet was much simpler than the ballista in its construction, so its wooden parts could be assembled and pegged together quickly. The pouch was made of leather.

FEROCIOUS FACTS

● The throwing arm could reach 60 ft (18 m) in length, giving great power.

● The enemy sent secret saboteurs to burn the much-feared trebuchet.

● A trebuchet could fling 2,000 stones in one day.

TERRIFYING TREBUCHET

The trebuchet launched much larger and more damaging missiles than the ballista. It could also fire from a greater distance. Its central mechanism was a lever similar to a seesaw that launched ammunition from a sling attached to the long end of a pole. Soldiers pulled this end down with a rope and loaded the sling with boulders and, later, bombs. The other end was a short arm weighed down with lead or a box of heavy sand or stones. This end crashed to the ground when the long arm was released, whipping the missile into the air.

WHERE
Middle East, Mediterranean, and Western Europe

WHEN
About 1100–1500

GRUESOME GREEK FIRE

WHERE
Mediterranean and
Middle East

WHEN
600–1500

Greek fire was a feared weapon aimed at wooden war machines, such as ships and siege towers. First used by Macedonian navies, it transformed warfare at sea. Greek fire was a violently explosive substance made from a secret petroleum mixture. It was heated, pressurized, and then fired with force through a siphon *(below)*. The flames could not be extinguished with water, much to the victims' horror. Greek fire machines were attached to ships' prows or set on top of ramparts to protect fortifications.

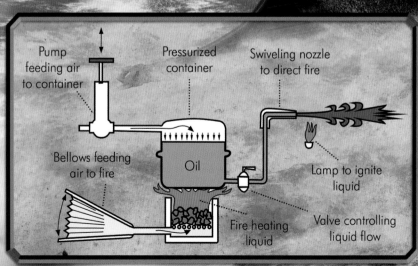

Pump feeding air to container

Pressurized container

Swiveling nozzle to direct fire

Bellows feeding air to fire

Oil

Lamp to ignite liquid

Fire heating liquid

Valve controlling liquid flow

GREAT BATTLES

In 941, the Rus (from present-day Russia), attacked Constantinople (now Istanbul) with 1,000 ships. The city's Byzantine defenders had only 15 galleys. But, armed with Greek fire projectors, they wiped out the Rus.

TOP TACTICS

Greek fire was used as a terror tactic, obliterating fleets and military machines. It burned crops so the enemy would starve. Many opponents fled as soon as they saw it.

MAKING THE MACHINE

Greek fire machines set on ships' prows were made of metal tubes and a funnel. A simpler, handheld metal siphon was used on shore. Round terracotta pots filled with Greek fire and sealed made effective grenades.

FEROCIOUS FACTS

- Greek fire could burn on water and stick to everything it touched.

- Only sand and vinegar could extinguish it.

- On Byzantine ships' prows, Greek fire was blown out through bronze lions' heads.

GREAT BATTLES

In 1453, at the Siege of Constantinople, Ottoman Turks blasted the city with a bombard made by Orban, a Hungarian. They stormed Constantinople, which they renamed Istanbul, and ended the great Byzantine Empire.

TOP TACTICS

Bombards were positioned to attack the weakest point of a fortification and to protect troops' positions. In 1494, Charles VIII of France wheeled a long line of bombards on carriages to invade Italy.

MAKING THE MACHINE

A bombard was made of iron bars welded into cylinders and connected with rings, or cast from bronze. It was strapped to a wooden frame with a back brace to stop the blast's kickback.

FEROCIOUS FACTS

• The biggest bombards had names. The Scottish bombard Mons Meg of 1449 got so hot it could not be fired continually.

• Great Turkish bombards of the 1400s hurled stone balls as heavy as tigers.

BOOMING MEDIEVAL BOMBARD

This small, heavy mortar was first designed to defend fortifications. It was soon used to blast holes in them and cause instant terror and destruction. The bombard operated with gunpowder instead of a mechanism. So it was able to blast heavy stone balls and showers of gravel faster and farther than before. Soldiers tied the bombard with rope to an angled platform and then rolled it into position. It was loaded through its muzzle, first with gunpowder and then with the missile. As the bombard became more reliable and destructive, hiding behind walls turned into a dangerous choice.

WHERE
China, Middle East, Mediterranean, and Europe

WHEN
About 1000–1500

Crushing Cannon

WHERE
China, Middle East,
Mediterranean, Europe,
then worldwide

WHEN
1100s–1900s

The cannon was large and strong enough to fire solid metal balls or hollow metal balls filled with sharp objects, lead shot, or explosives. It could be mounted on a ship or rolled or pulled by a horse onto the battlefield. Cannon could sink a fleet, blast a coastal defense, turn a fortress into rubble, or scatter an army. Later designs featured a spiral groove inside the cylindrical bore. This process was called rifling. It spun the missile, making its flight more stable and accurate. Explosives developed in power and reliability to make the cannon even more effective.

GREAT BATTLES

In 1588, the English navy fought off the great Spanish Armada. At first the English unsuccessfully fired cannon from afar at the armada's sails. Then they moved closer and fired broadside at the hulls, forcing the mighty Spanish fleet to withdraw.

TOP TACTICS

At sea, cannon that fired into wooden hulls wounded and killed enemy sailors with flying splinters. In a siege, attacking cannon were placed on top of trenches that protected the gunners below.

MAKING THE MACHINE

The cannon's bore cylinder was forged of bronze, iron, and steel, with reinforcing rings along its length. The metal was thicker at the explosives end. A long, thin fuse hole was bored into this end so the explosives could be ignited.

FEROCIOUS FACTS

• A cannon could weigh 8,000 lb (3,600 kg) and fire a 63-lb (28-kg) ball.

• In 1914, the German howitzer cannon, with a barrel that was 16.5 in (420 mm) wide, destroyed Liège, a Belgian city.

GREAT BATTLES

On November 20, 1917,
during World War I,
476 British tanks drove enemy
troops 3.5 miles (6 km) back
to the German-held city of
Cambrai.

TOP TACTICS

Tank attacks were planned
to shock, so they were
carried out without
warning signs such as air
bombardment. Shock tactics
became more successful
with World War II's faster
tanks, especially the Soviet
Union's BT series.

MAKING THE MACHINE

A tank's strong steel
chassis supported heavy
guns, a rear-mounted
engine, and a fuel tank.
The fully rotating turret,
first seen on the Renault
FT-17, was either cast or
welded.

FEROCIOUS FACTS

• The Renault FT
tank shown here was
lightweight and fast—and
feared for its ability to
change direction. Built in
1917, it was first operated
in World War I.

• The fearsome British
Mark IV fired with two
explosive cannon and four
machine guns, and was
also deployed toward the
end of World War I.

TANK ATTACK!

This armored vehicle houses powerful machine guns and explosive cannon that crush troops and demolish buildings. The tank was first built to shorten the duration of trench warfare, trample over barbed wire defenses, and put fear into armies and enemy populations. It combined advances in gun and engine design. Wide caterpillar tracks, first used on tractors, allowed tanks to move more easily than wheeled vehicles over mud, rocks, and trenches. The gunner aimed the machine gun in all directions through the tank's rotating turret. The driver operated the vehicle low down, behind protective plate armor.

WHERE
Europe, United States, then worldwide

WHEN
Late 1800s–present

Gunner

Machine gun

Swiveling turret

Emergency door

Fuel tank

Motor

Entrance

Driver

Speed lever

Tail

SILENT, SINISTER SUBMARINES

The submarine is a stealth machine, shaped to glide easily above or below water. Its hull's ballast chambers fill with either water or air to make it dive or rise. Submarines were first used to defend coastlines and ports, protecting ships laden with food supplies and raw materials. Later, the combined diesel-electric engine allowed submarines to sail across the open ocean, launching attacks on enemy shipping. The submarine's devastating torpedoes were aimed using coordinates given by a mechanical calculator. A gyrocompass, which used the rotation of Earth rather than magnetism, navigated the submarine underwater.

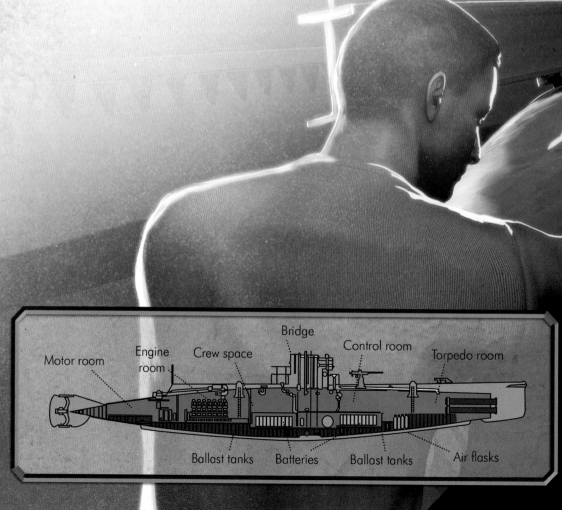

Motor room
Engine room
Crew space
Bridge
Control room
Torpedo room
Ballast tanks
Batteries
Ballast tanks
Air flasks

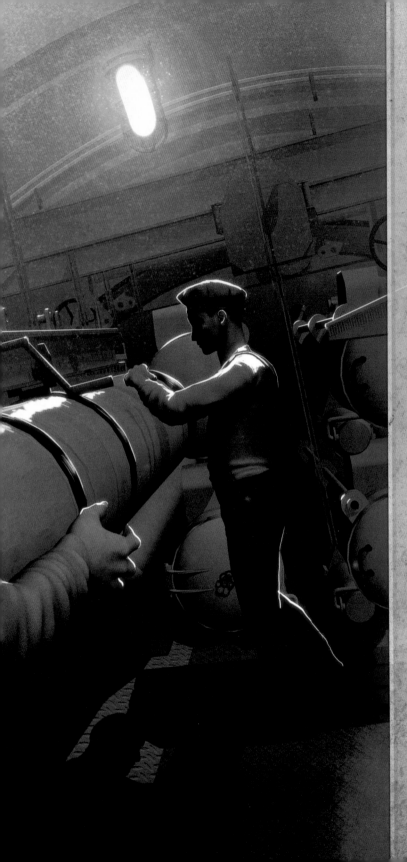

GREAT BATTLES

In both world wars, submarines did not engage in battles but quietly launched surprise attacks. They were forced to dive if their periscopes were spotted above water or their radio signals were detected.

TOP TACTICS

Submarines at first roamed on their own, picking off single ships undetected. But the ships began to sail in convoys protected by armed escorts. So submarines began to hunt in groups or "wolf packs."

MAKING THE MACHINE

This all-metal vessel's features included a chemical air-purification system. Waterproof partitions called bulkheads prevented flooding by separating the control room from the engine room and fore ends.

FEROCIOUS FACTS

• British M-class submarines could travel 5,000 miles (8,000 km) and fire from the turret with a 12-in (305-mm) gun.

• German U-boats sank over 13 million tons of shipping in World War I.

Into Battle with Mighty Machines

Dionysus of Syracuse and the Siege of Motya (398 BCE)

In this battle, Dionysus of Syracuse in Sicily laid the foundations for future siege warfare. He decided to attack Motya, an island city in western Sicily ruled by the North African Carthaginians. First, he built a bridge, or mole, to reach the city. Then he used catapults and siege towers to push back enemy fire from the fortification. Battering rams finally broke the city walls, and Dionysus's army stormed through.

Trebuchet Success at the Battle of Xiangyang (1267–1273)

The fearsome Mongol ruler Kublai Khan wanted to extend his Yuan empire by defeating the Chinese Song dynasty. The fortified twin cities of Fancheng and Xiangyang stood in his way. Kublai Khan's powerful cavalry could not charge through the heavily wooded region and attack the opposing forces. So siege warfare was his only hope. With machines that included cannon and simple trebuchets, he pummelled the cities' defenses. But the Song troops had prepared well, stringing netting around the fortifications. It was only when Kublai Khan brought in the more powerful counterweight trebuchet that Xiangyang finally fell in 1273. Kublai Khan now had a straight run along the Yangtze River.

CANNON FIRE AT THE SIEGE OF NAMUR (1914)

From the Middle Ages onward, cannon were widely used in land as well as sea battles. In 1692, French King Louis XIV broke the siege at the Belgian city of Namur with lines of cannon fire. Over 200 years later, during World War I (1914–1918), Namur was once more under siege. This time the enemy was Germany. By August 1914, Belgian troops had dug trenches and strung barbed wire between the forts that encircled Namur and protected it. With the promise of the French Fifth Army to support them, the Belgians felt secure. But by August 23, heavy German artillery had pounded both the forts and the city. A huge howitzer cannon called Big Bertha did much of the damage. Namur fell to more than 100,000 German troops. In World War II, unlucky Namur fell again.

STORMING TANKS AT CAMBRAI (1917)

The Battle of Cambrai in World War I was the first to demonstrate the power of tank warfare. In their first action at Flers in September 1916, during the Battle of the Somme, many tanks would not even start, and those that did became mired in mud. As a weapon of attack they had failed miserably. But in Cambrai, the British Tank Corps advanced 476 tanks in a surprise move across a 6-mile (10-km) front. Cavalry divisions, infantry, and 1,000 guns stood behind, ready to take advantage of a breakthrough. The tanks advanced, and on the first day alone 100 heavy guns and thousands of German soldiers were captured.

MORE FEROCIOUS FACTS

- Ancient Egyptian chariots charged at retreating troops in close formation, showering them with torrents of spears. When a fast-moving chariot overturned, the charioteers jumped out of the open back. Then they leaped onto the horses and galloped to safety.

- The most ancient ballista known is the Greek Scorpion from about 400 BCE. It shot huge arrows and bolts from a heavy wooden frame. The Scorpion was also known as the Shield Piercer because it could hit a shield from a long distance.

- There would be no bombards or cannon without gunpowder. The Chinese mixed the first gunpowder in the 800s CE. By 1259, arms manufacturers in the Chinese city of Qingzhou were making up to 2,000 cast-iron bombs every month.

- Above the deep river gorges in the Languedoc region of France, the fortress of Minerve hung on the edge of a limestone cliff. In 1210, Count Simon de Montfort pursued a religious group, the Cathars, to this hideaway. He loaded massive stones onto a long trebuchet and hurled them at the cliff face. The impact shook the fortress's well to pieces, leaving the Cathars without water. Minerve surrendered.

- Germany did not want the powerful United States of America to join World War I on the side of the Allies. But on May 7, 1915, one of Germany's U-boats sank the ocean liner *Lusitania*, killing 1,153 men, women, and children. They included 128 Americans. This affected public opinion in the United States, which joined the war in 1917.

- The British E-type submarine was built to dive safely to 100 ft (30 m). But during World War I, submarine E12 got caught in antisubmarine netting in the Dardanelles in Turkey. E12 was forced to dive to 245 ft (75 m), the deepest dive at the time. This well-built submarine survived.

GLOSSARY

BORE
Inside the cylinder of a cannon or gun

BROADSIDE
A ship's long side

BYZANTINE
Of the Eastern Roman Empire

CAST/CASTING
Making an object by pouring molten metal into a mold

CHASSIS
The frame carrying the body of a vehicle

FUSE
A length of cord that can be lit so a flame runs along its length

GYROCOMPASS
A nonmagnetic compass for finding direction underwater

MOLE
A bridge across a moat to a fortress

RAMPART
A defensive wall or bank

SABOTEUR
A secret, stealthy attacker

SINEW
Tough, stretchy animal tissue connecting muscle to bone

SIPHON
A tube along which a liquid can be forced

SMELTING
The process of melting metal from its ore using intense heat

SPOKED
A wheel fitted with rods connecting the rim to the hub

STEPPE
Vast grassland plain

INDEX

Alexander the Great 11
armies 6–7

ballistas 7, 7–8, 12–13, 16, 30
battering rams 10–11, 12, 13, 14
Battle of Cambrai 24, 29
Battle of Kadesh 8
Battle of Liège 23
Battle of Xiangyang 28
bombards 20–21, 30

cannon 7, 15, 22–23, 24, 25, 28, 29, 30
castles 10
chariots 6, 7, 8–9, 30
Charles VIII 20
Constantinople 19, 20

Demetrius I 15
Dionysus of Syracuse 28

fortified cities 7, 10, 20, 28
fortresses 7, 10, 11, 22, 30

great battles 6
Greek fire 18–19
gunpowder 6, 21, 30
gyrocompass 26

Helepolis 15
howitzer 23, 29

Kublai Khan 28

moles 28

scientific advances 6, 25
Siege of Constantinople 20
Siege of Jerusalem 12
Siege of Kenilworth Castle 15
Siege of Motya 28

Siege of Namur 29
Siege of Rhodes 15
Siege of Stirling Castle 16
Siege of Tyre 11
siege towers 7, 14–15, 18, 28
siege warfare 7, 10–11, 12, 14–15, 16, 20, 28, 30
Spanish Armada 23
submarines 26–27, 30

tanks 6, 24–25, 29
trebuchets 16–17, 28, 30

U-boats 27, 30

World War I 24–25, 27, 29, 30
World War II 29

THE AUTHOR

Catherine Chambers was born in Adelaide, South Australia, grew up in the UK, and studied African history and Swahili at the School of Oriental and African Studies in London. She has written about 130 books for children and young adults and enjoys seeking out intriguing facts for her nonfiction titles, which cover history, cultures, faiths, biography, geography, and the environment.

THE ILLUSTRATOR

Martín Bustamante is an illustrator and painter from Argentina. As a teenager, he found new and fascinating worlds full of color, shape, and atmosphere in movies such as *Star Wars* and the comic strip *Prince Valiant*, and these became his inspiration for drawing. As a professional illustrator, Martin has worked on books and magazines in Argentina, the United States, and Europe.

Picture Credits (abbreviations: t = top; b = bottom; c = center; l = left; r = right)

© www.shutterstock.com: com 6 bc, 7 tl, 7 bl

6 tr joyfull / Shutterstock.com